Curious George®

The Surprise Gift

Adaptation by Erica Zappy
Based on the TV series teleplay written by Raye Lankford

Houghton Mifflin Company, Boston 2008

For information about permission to reproduce selections from this book, write to Permissions, Houghton Mifflin Company, 215 Park Avenue South, New York, New York 10003.

Library of Congress Cataloging-in-Publication Data is on file
ISBN-13: 978-0-618-99864-7

Design by Afsoon Razavi
www.houghtonmifflinbooks.com

Printed in Singapore
TWP 10 9 8 7 6 5 4 3 2 1

George was a good little monkey and always very curious. This afternoon George was curious about a large box his friend was bringing home. A large box meant a large gift!

"Sorry, George," said his friend, setting the gift on the table. "This present's not for you. It's for Professor Wiseman's birthday. She'll open it at dinner tonight."

George was disappointed. Dinner was hours away. He wanted to know what was under the wrapping paper right now.

It was lucky George didn't have much time to think about the present.
His friend needed help preparing Professor Wiseman's birthday dinner.

"Here is something to unwrap," said his friend. "Peel this orange to get to the good stuff." George took the rind off — SQUIRT! The orange peel had kept the sweet juice inside.

George realized
there was a lot of food in
the kitchen that could be
unwrapped! Bananas, apples,
cheese, even an onion — stinky!
Soon George had unwrapped many
yummy things. Maybe too many . . .
But he still didn't know what was under the wrapping
paper of the gift.

Before George could let his curiosity get the best of him, his friend sent him to the department store to pick up his new suit.

At the store, George encountered many presents. There were gift boxes everywhere he looked, all brightly colored and too tempting for one little monkey to resist.

George unwrapped a box, but there was nothing interesting to him inside.

In the window display, there were more gift boxes. Strangely enough, the boxes had nothing at all inside. They were used for decoration . . . though not anymore!

Now George couldn't wait to help unwrap the present at home. He was sure it would have *something* inside. George hurried to finish his errand.

When George got home, the present was nowhere to be found! The man with the yellow hat had wisely hidden it from his curious little monkey. Did that stop George?

George looked under the table for the surprise gift. Then he went to check the bedrooms and the bathroom.

In the bathroom George noticed that the walls were covered in wrapping paper. George scratched. He peeled. He unwrapped. What did George find after all the unwrapping?

A wall! Unlike presents and fruit, nothing especially good was hiding underneath.

Luckily there was still something left to unwrap that promised something very nice (and very big) inside! It was time for Professor Wiseman to open her birthday gift.

With George's help she unwrapped and unwrapped and unwrapped.

Inside the big box was a small gift. "I never thought a present like this would be in such a big box," she said. The man with the yellow hat had wrapped it up so that she would have a harder time guessing what was inside. And it worked! George realized that what's on the outside doesn't always tell you what's on the inside!

But sometimes it does.

Matching Game

Match the following items to their wrappings.

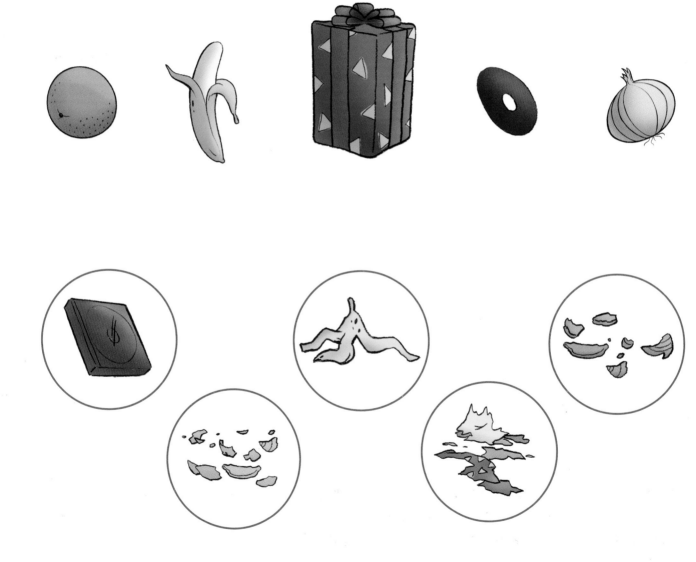

What's Inside?

Guessing Game

For this activity you will need scissors, tape and newspaper, wrapping paper, or old magazines. Find different-size boxes and containers in your house and put something inside. Then wrap them up! When you are finished wrapping, see if a parent or friend can guess what is inside. They can shake it, feel how heavy it is, and even ask twenty questions: Is it something I can eat? Is it bigger than a cookie? See how clues such as size and weight help you determine what you might find on the inside!

Think More About It

Can you find things in your house that are already "wrapped"? Do your favorite cookies come inside a bag? Maybe that bag is inside a box. What about your favorite cereal? And where do you keep your toys? Are they inside something else? Why do you think some things are wrapped?

Birthday Special

Draw a gift you'd like to get, and some of your favorite gifts to give:

Party Idea:

Wrap a party favor with many layers of paper (at least as many layers as the number of guests). On each layer write a funny fortune that you've come up with yourself. Each guest at your party can unwrap one layer and pass it to the next person. The person who unwraps the last layer gets to keep the prize, and everyone gets his or her fortune told!